Jumping in Puddles

by Liz Mills

**Illustrated by Carolyn Bracken
and Sandrina Kurtz**

Based on the books by Norman Bridwell

SCHOLASTIC INC.
New York Toronto London Auckland Sydney
Mexico City New Delhi Hong Kong Buenos Aires

It had rained the night before.

T-Bone saw puddles everywhere.

Today would be a good day to jump in puddles.

He decided to find his friends.

"Cleo, do you want to jump in puddles with me?" asked T-Bone.

"No," said Cleo. "I don't want to get wet and muddy. You go ahead, T-Bone."

"Okay," said T-Bone. "But I'm sorry you're not coming to play with me."

Then T-Bone went to visit Mac.

"Mac, would you come jump in puddles with me?" asked T-Bone.

"No," said Mac. "I want to take a nap. I'm sleepy." And Mac went back to sleep.

"Clifford, will you jump in puddles with me?" asked T-Bone.

"I'd like to," said Clifford. "But I won't fit in a puddle."

"You can still play. I've got an idea!" said T-Bone.

And so they walked to the park.

"Isn't this fun, Clifford?" asked T-Bone as he slid off Clifford's tail and jumped into a puddle.

"Yes, it's lots of fun," said Clifford. "I'm glad we're puddle jumping together."

Just then, Cleo walked into the park.

"Hi, T-Bone," said Cleo. "Hi, Clifford."

"Didn't you want to stay dry, Cleo?" asked T-Bone.

"I did want to stay dry," said Cleo. "But I didn't want to be by myself."

Mac walked into the park.

"Hi, T-Bone," said Mac.
"Hi, Clifford. Hi, Cleo."

"Didn't you want to take a nap, Mac?" asked T-Bone.

"I'm not tired anymore. And now I would like to jump into puddles!"

Puddle jumping is
best with friends!